adapted by David Lewman
based on the teleplay by Peter Egan
illustrated by Sharon Ross
with Anastasios Gionis and Carl A. Braxton

SCHOLASTIC INC.

New York Toronto London Auckland Sydney
Mexico City New Delhi Hong Kong Buenos Aires

ISBN 0-439-40584-X

12 11 10 9 8 7 6 5 4 3 2 1   2 3 4 5 6 7/0

Printed in the U.S.A.

First Scholastic printing, September 2002

Based on the TV series Rugrats® created by Arlene Klasky, Gabor Csupo, and Paul Germain as seen on Nickelodeon ®

"Tommy," Chuckie said nervously, "why does your house look so a-scary?"

Tommy looked around. "I don't know, Chuckie, but big stuffs is goin' on."

"You babies don't know nothin'," Angelica scoffed. "It's 'cause tonight is Hallomean!"

"Oh, that's right," Tommy said. "Uh, what's Hallomean?"

"Hallomean is when you dress up and get lotsa candy!" Angelica twirled around in her sparkly dress. "I'm gonna be a princess 'cause they get the most candy."

"Do we all get to be princesses?" asked Chuckie hopefully.

"Nope," said Angelica. "I heard your mommy say you're gonna be a *werewuff*!"

"A werewuff!" squeaked Chuckie. "What's a werewuff?"

Angelica adjusted her crown. "Oh, just a mean, scary monster with a hairy face and pointy ears that gets hunted down in the forest!" Angelica narrowed her eyes. "And the best part about Hallomean is, whatever you dress up as, you turn into . . . for *real*."

"You m-mean—," Chuckie stammered.

"That's right, 'Fraidy Cat Finster," said Angelica. "Tonight you're gonna turn into a werewuff forever and ever!"

While Chuckie took his afernoon nap he dreamed he was a werewolf.

"No!" Chuckie cried out. "NOOOOOOO!"

Chuckie's eyes popped open. "Whew!" he said. "It was only a nightscare."

Then he heard a strange cackling sound. "Kimi?" Chuckie asked. "Is that you?"

"There is no more Kimi!" Kimi screeched. "There is only Kimi-Witch!"

"Oh, no!" cried Chuckie. "Angelica was right!"

Just then Chuckie's dad came in. "Happy Halloween!" he said. "Where's my little werewolf?"

Later, everyone gathered at Screamland.

"I don't wanna be a werewuff, Angelica," Chuckie said sadly. "I want to be myself again."

"What do I look like?" she answered. "Some kind of magical princess?"

"Um . . . yes," said Chuckie. "You do."

Angelica smirked. "Hmm . . . you don't say. Okay, Finster, I'll change you little monsters back into dumb babies *if* you all give me your tricka-treat candy."

TRICK-OR-TREAT STREET

HAUNTED HOUSE

HAUNTED FOREST

WELCOME TO SCREA

Phil and Lil screeched like bats.

Tommy pulled his cape over his face. "We like bein' monsters!" he said.

Chuckie sighed. "I'll give you my candy," he said.

"That's not good enough," growled Angelica. "You *all* hafta gimme your candy, or *nobody* gets turned back into a crybaby!"

Grandpa Lou and Lulu took the babies into the kiddie haunted house.

"What good is a mirror if it doesn't show how beautiful you are?" Angelica said, bored. "I'm gonna go find a *real* haunted house for big kids like me."

"Wait!" cried Chuckie. "I need you to change me back into myself first!"

But Angelica was already gone.

Chuckie saw another girl dressed as a princess. Just as he was about to ask her to change him back, she saw his reflection in the mirror and screamed.

"I'm stuck as a mean, scary monster forever!" Chuckie cried, and he ran out of the haunted house.

The babies found Chuckie sitting outside the haunted forest. "Well, guys, I guess this is good-bye," said Chuckie. "Since I'm a werewuff now, I gots to go live in the forest." He sighed. "'Cept I'm too a-scared to go in there."

"You don't have to go," said Tommy. "We're going to get lotsa candy and give it to Angelica so she'll turn us back into babies."

"You are?" asked Chuckie, perking up. "You're the bestest friends ever!"

HAUNTED FOREST

The babies went straight to Trick-or-Treat Street. Tommy knocked on a door, and a ghost opened it and filled Tommy's bag with candy.

"An extra-scary werewolf should get extra candy," said the ghost, pouring even more candy into Chuckie's bag.

"Now we gots to find Angelica!" said Kimi.

"I see her!" cried Kimi, pointing to a dark haunted house.

"W-W-We're gonna g-go in th-th-there?" stammered Chuckie.

"Yup," said Tommy. "'Member, you guys, we're monsters now. So nothin' can a-scare us!"

They finally found Angelica outside the haunted house, huddled under a tree. "Angelica!" called Tommy. "We got your candy!"

The babies held up their bags.

"I don't care about your stupid candy!" Angelica cried. "Just get me out of this crazy place!"

Chuckie couldn't believe his pointed ears. "First you gotta turn us back into babies," he said.

"First you gotta get me outta here!" hissed Angelica.

"NO!" Chuckie shouted. "I'm sicka being a-scared and sicka being a werewuff! So make like a princess, and turn me into Chuckie again!"

"All right!" said Angelica. "I'll do it!" She waved her arms and chanted, "*Finster-dee, Finster-dah, make them dumb babies again, blah, blah, blah!*"

The babies felt like babies again. But the graveyard seemed much scarier. "Now what do we do?" asked Kimi.

"I 'member what it's like to be a werewuff," said Chuckie. "Follow me!"

Chuckie led the babies past the gravestones. Whenever a pretend zombie popped up, Chuckie howled like a werewolf and ran on.

But then they reached a dead end. "We're trapped, Finster. Trapped!" wailed Angelica.

Chuckie stepped backward and . . .

. . . they all fell down a tunnel!

The babies landed on an inflatable mat below.

"That was great, Chuckie!" said Tommy. "You were brave even though you're not a werewuff anymore!"

"You were never monsters," said Angelica, gloating. "I tricked you!"

Phil looked puzzled. "But if Chuckie wasn't a werewuff, how'd he get so brave?"

"Maybe I'm still a werewuff," said Chuckie, worried.

Just then the little girl from the kiddie haunted house sneaked up behind Chuckie. "BOO!" she screamed, and Chuckie jumped up in the air.

He sighed, and then he smiled. "I guess I really *am* Chuckie again."